KOLOBOK

SIÂN VALVIS

DOVILĖ ČIAPAITĖ

For my parents

Once upon a time in a land not far away,
Lived an old man and his wife who was just as old and grey.

High upon a hilltop, a step beyond the wood,
Underneath the birches, their little cottage stood.

"Bake me a little bun, Old Girl?" asked the man one day.
"From what? We have no flour left!" she said, to his dismay.

"Just rummage round the granary and gather up the crumbs,
You're sure to find enough for one delicious little bun."

The woman did just so, she scratched and scraped up all the flour,
She added in the sour cream and kneaded for an hour,
And rolled it all into a bun, a round and sunny fellow,
She fried the bun – the *kolobok* – till he was golden yellow.

She teetered on the wooden stool and laid him on the sill,
She made sure he was comfortable and left him there to chill.

Alas, the little kolobok got bored of lying down,
He rolled and rolled and rolled until he landed on the ground.

KOLOBOK...

From windowsill to bench and from bench onto the floor,
He was aiming for the courtyard as he bounded through the door.

As the little kolobok rolled along his way,
He came upon a **hare** who turned to him to say:

"Oh, little Kolobok! I'll eat you up in one!"
"No you don't, you cheeky Hare! Not till you've heard my song!"

As the hare listened on,
The kolobok began his song:
"I'm a little kolobok – a jolly, little bun!
In the granary they scraped me,
Out of crumbs they patacaked me,
Into sour cream they dipped me,
In the frying pan they flipped me,
On the windowsill they slipped me,
But Grandpa couldn't catch me,
And Grandma couldn't snatch me,
You can try to eat me, too,
But Hare – I'm too smart for you!"

And off went the kolobok

till he was out of sight

As the little kolobok rolled along his way,
He came upon a **wolf** who turned to him to say:

"Oh, little Kolobok! I'll eat you up in one!"
"No you won't, you grey, old Wolf! Not till you've heard my song!"

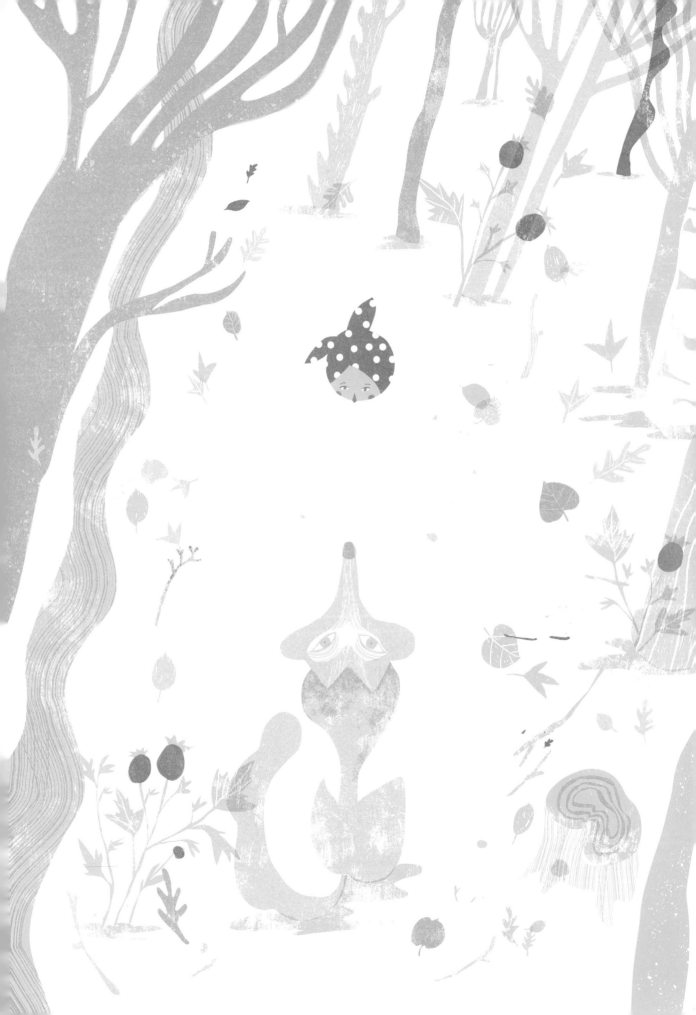

Then, before the wolf had time,
The kolobok began his rhyme:
"I'm a little kolobok – a roly, poly bun!
In the granary they scraped me,
Out of crumbs they patacaked me,
Into sour cream they dipped me,
In the frying pan they flipped me,
On the windowsill they popped me,
But Grandpa couldn't stop me,
And Grandma couldn't snatch me,
And Hare couldn't catch me,
You can try to eat me, too,
But Wolfy – I'm too smart for you!"

And off went the kolobok

till he was out of sight

The kolobok continued through the woods without a care,
When crashing through the bushes came a great big bolshie **bear**.

"Oh, little Kolobok! I'll eat you up in one!"
"No you can't, you clumsy Bear! Not till you've heard my song!"

As the bear was sitting pretty,
Kolobok began his ditty:
"I'm a little kolobok — a happy, scrappy bun!
In the granary they scraped me,
Out of crumbs they patacaked me,
Into sour cream they dipped me,
In the frying pan they flipped me,
On the windowsill they popped me,
But Grandpa couldn't stop me,
And Grandma couldn't snatch me,
And Hare couldn't catch me,
Wolfy tried to eat me,
You can try to eat me, too,
But Bear — I'm just too smart for you!"

And off went the kolobok

till he was out of sight

As the little kolobok rolled along his way,
He came upon a wily **fox** who turned to him to say:

"Well, goodness me! Who could this be? This fine and dandy fellow!
I dare say it's a kolobok — all soft and golden yellow."

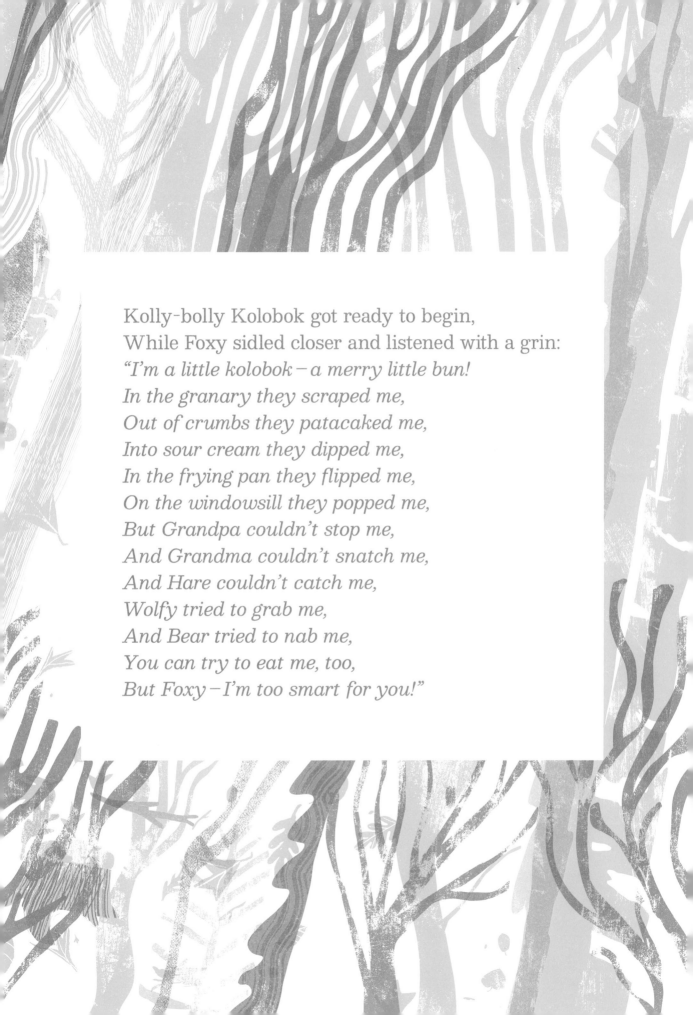

Kolly-bolly Kolobok got ready to begin,
While Foxy sidled closer and listened with a grin:
"I'm a little kolobok – a merry little bun!
In the granary they scraped me,
Out of crumbs they patacaked me,
Into sour cream they dipped me,
In the frying pan they flipped me,
On the windowsill they popped me,
But Grandpa couldn't stop me,
And Grandma couldn't snatch me,
And Hare couldn't catch me,
Wolfy tried to grab me,
And Bear tried to nab me,
You can try to eat me, too,
But Foxy – I'm too smart for you!"

"Well, isn't that a splendid song!" said Foxy, drawing near,
"But since I'm old, I hate to say, I'm struggling to hear.
Perhaps, my little Kolobok, allow me to propose,
You sing your song, just one more time, but this time on my nose?"

Delighted was the kolobok, so proud of what he'd sung,
With a mighty little jump onto Fox's nose he sprung:

"I'm a little kolobok – a jolly little bun..."

When – "**GULP!**" went the wily fox and ate him up in one!

Thank you to
Robert Chandler, Dovilė Čiapaitė,
Fontanka, Bureau Bureau, Fabio Alher,
and my family.

Kolobok is a Slavic folktale, thought to have originated in the
19th century, similar to *The Gingerbread Man* in English tradition.
Kolobok is well known in Russia and many other countries in Europe.
Each culture has its own version—sometimes *Kolobok* manages to
escape in the end, and sometimes he's not so lucky! Like all folktales,
Kolobok offers a glimpse into the magic and mysticism of another world.

Adapted by Siân Valvis
Illustrated by Dovilė Čiapaitė
Edited by Mark Sutcliffe and Frank Althaus
Designed by Bureau Bureau

Published in 2021
ISBN: 978-1-906257-41-5

Fontanka
5A Bloomsbury Square
London WC1A 2TA
www.fontanka.co.uk

Set in Besley* 14pt by Owen Earl.
Printed with Pantone inks 565-u, 707-u, and 128-u.
Printed in Vilnius by Balto Print on 140 GSM Maestro.

This book has been selected to receive financial assistance from English PEN's
"PEN Translates!" programme, supported by Arts Council England. English PEN exists
to promote literature and our understanding of it, to uphold writers' freedoms around the
world, to campaign against the persecution and imprisonment of writers for stating their
views, and to promote the friendly co-operation of writers and the free exchange of ideas.
www.englishpen.org